TEAM SPIRIT

Eric Stevens

illustrated by Tuesday Mourning

Librarian Reviewer
Chris Kreie, Media Specialist

Reading Consultant
Mary Evenson, Teacher

www.raintreepublishers.co.uk
Visit our website to find out
more information about
Raintree books.

To order:
☎ Phone 0845 6044371
🖷 Fax +44 (0) 1865 312263
🖳 Email myorders@capstonepub.co.uk

Customers from outside the UK please telephone +44 1865 312262

Raintree is an imprint of Capstone Global Library Limited, a company incorporated in
England and Wales having its registered office at 7 Pilgrim Street, London, EC4V 6LB –
Registered company number: 6695582

"Raintree" is a registered trademark of Pearson Education Limited, under licence to
Capstone Global Library Limited

Text © Stone Arch Books 2009
First published by Stone Arch Books in 2009
First published in hardback and paperback in the United Kingdom by
Capstone Global Library in 2010
The moral rights of the proprietor have been asserted.

Edited in the United Kingdom by Diyan Leake
Original illustrations © Stone Arch Books 2009
Illustrated by Tuesday Mourning
Originated by Capstone Global Library Ltd
Printed in China by Leo paper Products Ltd

ISBN 978 1 406 21382 9 (hardback)
14 13 12 11 10
10 9 8 7 6 5 4 3 2 1

ISBN 978 1 406 21403 1 (paperback)
14 13 12 11 10
10 9 8 7 6 5 4 3 2 1

British Library Cataloguing in Publication Data
Stevens, Eric – Team spirit
A full catalogue record for this book is available from the British Library.

CONTENTS

CHAPTER 1

BAD NEWS

Anna Reed crouched slightly in the goal and squinted up the pitch. She smiled as she watched Bethany West kick the football down the empty pitch they used for practice. Bethany was a great ball handler. She was also Anna's best friend.

"You can't stop me!" Bethany yelled as she moved closer to the goal.

Anna watched Bethany's feet carefully. She stayed ready to pounce.

Bethany was tricky. She'd make goalies think she was shooting low. Then she would go high with her shot. She was also good at faking left, then shooting right.

Bethany planted her left foot and got ready to shoot. Anna bent down and bounced slightly, ready to block. It looked like Bethany was shooting right.

Then Bethany kicked. At the last second, Anna realized the shot was going left. She leaped across the goal. Just before the ball flew into the net, Anna was able to tap it with her left hand. It went off course and missed the net.

Anna hit the ground hard, but she was smiling. She stood up and brushed the dirt off her T-shirt and shorts.

"Nice shot, Bethany," Anna said to her friend. "But not nice enough."

"How'd you know I was going left?" Bethany asked. "I was sure you'd think I was going right."

Anna shrugged. "Just psychic, I guess," she said, smiling. "Anyway, that was a great shot. East Moor doesn't stand a chance this year!" East Moor Secondary School was their school's biggest rival in girls' football.

"Especially with you in goal!" Bethany replied.

Anna sighed. "Looks like it's getting late," she said. "I'd better get home."

Bethany nodded. "Yeah," she said. "Dinner's probably waiting for me, too."

"See you tomorrow," Anna said.

Bethany rolled her eyes. "First day of school," she said. "Oh joy."

Anna waved. Then she jogged home.

"Dad!" Anna called as she came into her house. "I'm home!"

She walked into the living room. Her dad put down his newspaper. "There's post for you," he said. "From school."

"From school?" Anna said, worried. A letter from school was usually bad news, but the term hadn't even started yet.

"Have a seat," Dad said.

He picked up a letter from the coffee table in front of him. After a quick glance at it, he handed it to Anna.

"Who is it from?" Anna asked.

"Well, read it!" Dad replied.

Anna read the letter. It was from Miss Johnson, the girls' football coach.

"What?" Anna yelled as she reached the last line. "I can't believe this!"

"I know," Dad replied. "I can understand why you'd be upset."

"I have to call Bethany!" Anna replied.

Dad nodded. "Okay," he said. "Try to be quick, though. Dinner's ready."

Anna ran up to her bedroom and quickly dialled Bethany's house. "Did you hear?" Anna practically yelled into the phone.

"Hear what?" Bethany replied.

"Didn't you get a letter from school today?" Anna said. "About funding for PE?"

"Yes, I did," Bethany said. "What are we going to do? No funding means no girls' football team this year!"

* CHAPTER 2 *

COMBINED?

"This is the worst news ever," Jasmine Khan said the next day at lunch. She stared down at her green beans. Jasmine was the best defender on the Gladstone Secondary School girls' football team, the Eagles.

Even though Jasmine was much taller than Anna and Bethany, she was like a little sister to them. They were all in Year 9, but Jasmine had been moved up a year and was a year younger.

"Jasmine's right!" Anna said. "How are we going to survive school without the football team?" she asked.

"There's Miss Johnson!" Jasmine said. She jumped up and walked over to the coach. Anna and Bethany followed her.

"Miss Johnson!" Anna called.

"Hi, girls," the coach replied. She looked worried and upset.

"Miss, tell us what's going on!" Jasmine said. "No girls' football team this year?"

Miss Johnson frowned. "I'm afraid that's right, Jasmine," she replied. "We just couldn't afford to have a girls' football team at Gladstone this year."

"But there's going to be a boys' team!" Anna pointed out. "That's not fair!"

Miss Johnson shook her head. "I know," she said, "but some players from East Moor are joining because their funding was cut as well. The girls' team would have only had you three, plus Sophie and Kate. That's not even enough for a starting line-up. We probably would have had to cancel the team anyway, even without the funding cut. All the schools in the county are being affected."

"But we want to play!" Anna said.

"Yeah!" Bethany added.

Miss Johnson sighed. "I know. I think we've figured something out," she replied. "I'm on my way to meet with Mr Stewart right now about an idea that might work." The coach patted Anna on the shoulder and tried to smile. Then she walked off towards the headteacher's office.

As Anna, Bethany, and Jasmine sat in their lesson an hour later, their teacher made an announcement to the class.

"Could I please have your attention," Mrs Wilde said. "Any girls who wish to play football this season should meet with Miss Johnson immediately after school today."

Their teacher continued, "Due to a lack of funds for football at our school and East Moor Secondary School, the teams have been combined."

"What?" half the class said at once.

"No way," Jasmine said.

Anna's mouth hung open. "We have to play with East Moor," she said. "Our biggest rivals!"

CHAPTER 3

ENEMIES

Anna, Bethany, and Jasmine sat by the window in their last class of the day. Anna stared out the window at the football pitch.

"It's not much of a pitch," she thought. The grass was mostly brown or gone completely. Even from where she was sitting, she could see rocky patches on the pitch. The goal posts were bent and their nets were torn and falling off in places.

"Anna," Bethany said. "Wake up."

"Huh?" Anna replied, turning away from the window. "Is it time to go?"

Bethany shook her head. "No," she replied, "but you were daydreaming. We have to finish this project."

"I know," Anna said. "Just thinking about football. I'll miss playing on our pitch."

"That nasty old pitch?" Bethany said, nodding towards the window. "You're crazy."

Anna shrugged. "Whatever," she said.

"I'm excited about playing at East Moor," Bethany went on in a whisper. "Remember how nice their pitch is?"

"Of course," Anna said, thinking about their rival's perfect sports field.

Jasmine turned around in her seat.

"Talking about the football team?" she asked.

Anna and Bethany nodded. Bethany was smiling, but Anna seemed a little down.

"Are you worried, Anna?" Jasmine asked. "Me too."

"What are you worried about?" Bethany asked.

"Are you kidding?" Jasmine replied. "It's East Moor School! Our enemies! What if their players don't even want us around?"

Anna opened her eyes wide. "Whoa," she said. "I hadn't even thought of that."

Suddenly, Bethany wasn't smiling either.

After the bell rang, the girls grabbed their bags and darted from the classroom.

Mr Conrad barely had time to call after them, "Don't forget! Page 10 in your textbook, for tomorrow!"

"Ugh," Bethany said as she jogged towards Miss Johnson's office. "Homework already."

The coach was waiting for them in her office, along with Sophie and Kate.

"Hi, Soph," Anna said with a wave. "Hi, Kate."

The other girls smiled and said hello. Then Miss Johnson clapped her hands. "Okay, girls," she said. "Let's get to the minibus."

"Take a deep breath, everybody," Bethany said. "We're going where no Gladstone girl has gone before."

* CHAPTER 4 *

GLADSTONE GIRLS

The minibus pulled up in front of East Moor School. All the girls stared out of the windows.

East Moor Secondary School was huge, and it looked brand new. It was all concrete and big windows. It was set on a big green field of grass. Green hills rose up behind it.

"Here we are," Miss Johnson said as the driver opened the door. "Everyone out." The girls got out and stood around their coach.

"All right, everyone," Miss Johnson said. "We're guests here at East Moor, so be good."

The girls all nodded.

"And one more thing," she added as they started walking towards the entrance. "We may be at East Moor now, but you'll always be Gladstone girls to me. Okay?"

The girls all smiled. They followed Miss Johnson through the school towards the big field where the football pitch was. Miss Johnson pushed open the big metal doors and the five teammates stepped outside.

The East Moor School football pitch was bright green. The boundaries and halfway line were all freshly painted. The goal posts looked brand new.

All around the pitch were stands for students, teachers, and families to watch games. Girls' football was very important at East Moor Secondary School.

"Football is way more important here than at Gladstone," Anna muttered to herself.

"What?" Bethany whispered.

Anna shook her head. "Nothing," she replied. Then she nodded towards the pitch. "Look over there."

The East Moor players were all gathered on the pitch. There were about fifteen of them, and they were all wearing the East Moor football kit.

"They look like they're in an advert," Bethany whispered.

The football kits were bright yellow, with red and white numbers and red and white stripes on the sleeves and shorts.

One person among the East Moor team was wearing a red warm-up jacket and jogging bottoms. She was about the same height as the players, but her hair was very short and bright white. "That must be their coach," Jasmine said.

Kate nodded. "Yep," she said. "I hear she's pretty tough."

"Miss Johnson?" the coach called. She waved. "Come on over!"

The girls followed Miss Johnson towards the middle of the pitch. The East Moor girls watched as the Gladstone girls walked up. Anna thought that the East Moor players didn't seem happy to have guests.

"Hi," Miss Johnson said as she shook the other coach's hand. "Call me Miss J."

"All right, Miss J," said the other coach. "I'm Coach Suzy."

Bethany leaned over to Kate. "Coach Suzy?" she whispered. "Sounds tough."

The other girls giggled. Miss Johnson shot them a look and they quieted down.

"Well, Coach Suzy," Miss Johnson said, "here are your new players from Gladstone Secondary School."

Coach Suzy turned to the Gladstone girls and wrinkled her brow. "Hmm," she said. "Looks like a good bunch."

Then Coach Suzy squinted at Anna. "Aren't you Anna Reed?" she said. "And you're Bethany West, right?"

Anna and Bethany looked at each other. "Yes," they replied together.

A couple of girls from the East Moor team stepped forward. They looked at Anna and Bethany.

Coach Suzy smiled at Anna and Bethany. "I remember you two from last year," she said. "For some reason, I thought you were in Year 9 last year, from how well you played. But now I remember that you were in Year 8."

The two girls from East Moor who had moved to the front looked at each other. Then they whispered something.

"Yes," Anna said. "We're in Year 9 now."

"Great," Coach Suzy said. "East Moor will be lucky to have you."

"Right," said the taller of the two whispering East Moor girls. "Very lucky." She glared at Anna.

* CHAPTER 5 *

LUCK

"Okay," Coach Suzy said. She blew her whistle. "Let's get started with the trials!"

The East Moor girls all ran to one end of the pitch. "Okay," Jasmine said. "I guess we should go with them." The five Gladstone girls ran after the others.

"Everyone line up," Coach Suzy called. "We're going to do some dribbling drills, some passing drills, some shooting drills, and then a practice match."

Anna glanced at one of the girls who had been whispering. The girl was tall and had long blonde hair. Her jersey said the name "Rivers."

"That's Lindsay Rivers," said Sophie in her ear. "She's the goalie. She started last year, too, just like you."

Anna nodded. "Cool," she said.

"And with her, that's Alicia Lee," Sophie added. Alicia was short and had straight black hair. "She's a defender. Not great, but she did start last year."

"Think she'll be competition for Jasmine?" Anna asked.

Sophie bit her lip. "Hm," she said. "Maybe. Jasmine is better, if you ask me, and really tough. But maybe Coach Suzy will treat her own players better."

Anna nodded. "Yeah," she said.

The drills went on for almost an hour. Then the practice match started.

"Anna," Coach Suzy called out once the girls had gathered around. "You're goalie for team A. Lindsay, you're on team B."

Lindsay glared at Anna with a smirk and mouthed at her, "You're finished."

"Bring it on," Anna mouthed back.

"Yeah!" Bethany called to Lindsay. "We'll see who's finished!"

"Okay, enough of that," Coach Suzy said with a little chuckle. "Team A, throw on some blue jerseys, and let's get going."

All the Gladstone girls were placed on team A. Anna was relieved. She knew how her old teammates played, and what to expect.

Bethany took a pass off the kick-off and headed down the pitch. Anna smiled.

"Think she'll score on Lindsay?" Jasmine said from her position near the crease.

"Yeah, definitely!" Anna called back. "She was the best scorer in the league!"

The girls watched as Bethany dodged two defenders, including Alicia. "Here comes the shot," Anna said. "Watch. She's going high in the right corner."

Anna was right, but Lindsay didn't expect it. She leapt high to the left.

"Goal!" Jasmine called, running up to midfield to give Bethany a hug. "Nice one!"

"Celebrate later, please," Coach Suzy said over team A's cheering. Then she grabbed the ball and dropped it in the middle for the kick-off.

Lindsay wasn't fooled again by Bethany, or anyone else. But Anna didn't let in even one goal, so Lindsay's one mistake lost the game. Team A won 1–0.

While Jasmine, Bethany, and Anna were talking after the game, Lindsay and Alicia walked over to them.

"Lucky shot, Bethany," Lindsay said. "It won't happen again."

"Lucky?" Bethany said, looking Lindsay up and down. "That was not luck."

Alicia rolled her eyes. Then she and Lindsay walked off.

"Nice game to you too," Anna muttered as the two other girls walked away.

"Don't worry about her," another East Moor girl said. She was about Anna's height, and had curly dark hair.

"She's just worried because she's actually got some competition in goal this year," the girl went on. "I'm Caitlin, by the way."

"Hi, Caitlin," Anna said. "I'm Anna, and this is Jasmine and Bethany. And that's Sophie and Kate over there."

Caitlin nodded. "I know who you guys are," she said. "I wasn't on the team last year, but I went to the games. I saw you two play a few times. You're really great."

"Thanks," Bethany said. "You were pretty good out there today too."

"I hope so," Caitlin said. "It'll be fun playing offence with you if I make the starting line-up."

Suddenly Coach Suzy blew two sharp blasts on her whistle. All the girls gathered around her.

"Nice job, team A," Coach Suzy said. "I was really impressed with everyone today. And I'll post the line-up by Thursday afternoon." She smiled.

"Gladstone girls," she went on, "Miss J will post the results up at your school then too. Now go and have a shower, everyone."

The sun started to set as the Gladstone minibus bounced along towards their school. "Boy, Lindsay Rivers is not my favourite person," Bethany said.

"Don't let her get to you," Anna said. "Besides, I'm the one who's competing with her for starting goalie."

"You'll get it for sure, Anna," Jasmine said.

"Definitely," Bethany added. "The three of us will all be starting. That's for sure."

· CHAPTER 6 ·

THE LINE-UP

The next few days were tough. Even though Anna, Bethany, and Jasmine were confident, they didn't know for certain they would make the team. And they really didn't know if they'd get to be on the starting line-up.

"It's just not fair," Bethany said. She was pacing in front of the notice board near the changing rooms. They were waiting for Miss Johnson to put up the list.

"I mean, if we had a Gladstone team this year," Bethany went on, "we'd all be starters . . . easy!"

The others watched Bethany walk back and forth. "You said that already," Jasmine said. "And you're making me nervous with all your walking back and forth, and back and forth, and back and forth."

"Nervous?" Anna joked. "You're making me dizzy!"

Everyone laughed, except for Bethany.

"How could you be anything but nervous?" Bethany said. "Or sick? I'm both!"

"Try to relax," Anna said. "Miss Johnson will be here with the list any minute now."

"I can't relax," Bethany said. "I have to keep moving."

"Hi, girls," Miss Johnson said suddenly. "I think I have what you're waiting for!"

"How does it look?" Bethany asked. She leaned over Miss Johnson's shoulder as she put up the list. The other girls jumped up and ran over to the board.

"I think you'll all be pretty pleased," Miss Johnson said. She smiled and stood back.

"We all made it!" Jasmine said.

"Yes!" Sophie said.

"And you're starting on defence, Jasmine," Kate pointed out.

"And I'm starting in midfield!" Bethany shouted.

"I'm not surprised," Jasmine said, giving Bethany a hug.

"What about me?" Anna said, trying to get a look at the list from behind her friends.

"Of course you made it," Bethany said. "And . . . oh."

"Oh?" Anna said, finally checking out the list. "What do you mean, oh?"

Anna looked down the list of names. She had made the team, all right. But there it was, in black and white: "Starting goalie: Lindsay Rivers."

CHAPTER 7

UNFAIR

"I can't believe this," Jasmine said. The Gladstone girls were sitting on their minibus on the way to East Moor for practice. "It's totally unfair!"

"Unfair?" Bethany said. She bounced out of her seat as the minibus hit a bump. "It's more than unfair!"

Kate shook her head. "I thought for sure Anna would start after Lindsay let in that goal of yours, Bethany," she said.

Bethany gritted her teeth. "Aren't you angry, Anna?" she asked.

Anna shrugged. She was disappointed, but she didn't want to let herself get angry. "I guess I'm a little angry," she finally said.

"Miss Johnson!" Bethany called to the front of the minibus. "Can you do anything about this?"

Miss Johnson smiled weakly and shook her head. "Sorry, girls," she said. "I'm disappointed too, but I'm not the coach anymore. There's nothing I can do."

"You're still our coach," Jasmine said. "I mean, like you said, we're still Gladstone girls, right?"

Miss Johnson nodded. "Of course, and I'm still the Gladstone coach. But when it comes to East Moor, I don't have any power at all."

"None?" Anna said. "We all thought you were the second coach!"

Miss Johnson laughed lightly. "Nope," she said. "I'll be coming to as many practices with you girls as I can, because I care about you and love to watch you play and win! But you're at East Moor this year, which means you're Coach Suzy's team. And she's the only coach you have."

Anna slumped in her seat.

When the Gladstone girls arrived at the football pitch, the East Moor girls were in their kits and waiting. Lindsay and Alicia ran over to Anna right away.

"So, Second String," Lindsay said to Anna with a sneer, "decided to show up?"

"Of course I showed up," Anna said. "I'm on the team. Why wouldn't I?"

Alicia laughed and Lindsay shushed her with a wicked smile.

"Oh, I don't know," Lindsay said, looking back at Anna. "I'm not sure I'd show up if I were you."

"Watch it, Lindsay," Bethany said, stepping up. Lindsay glared at her.

"Just leave me alone, Lindsay, okay?" Anna replied. She turned away and started to do some stretches, trying to look like Lindsay's comments hadn't bothered her.

The truth was, though, they had.

CHAPTER 8

SECOND STRING

East Moor's first game came quickly. After a week of training, Anna and her friends were starting to feel at home.

Lindsay and Alicia had even stopped teasing them so much. Still, Anna sometimes caught the two East Moor girls whispering and looking at her.

Before the first game was about to start, Anna sat on the East Moor bench.

Caitlin was kicking the ball around in front of the goal. She spotted Anna on the bench. "Hi," Caitlin said as she sat down next to Anna.

"Hi, Caitlin," Anna replied. "Nice shot. It was a really good one."

"Thanks," said Caitlin. "I've seen Lindsay play so many times, I know all her problems. She's easy for me to score on."

"Are you starting today?" Anna asked.

"Yep," Caitlin said. "Right wing."

Anna nodded. She watched Jasmine and Bethany pass the ball, while Sophie and Kate tried to stop them.

"Don't worry about it, Anna," Caitlin said. "I'm sure Coach Suzy will let you play today. She just knows Lindsay so well. She's seen her play so many times."

"I suppose so," Anna said, looking at her feet. She tried to smile. When she looked up at the pitch again, Lindsay and Alicia were standing in their goal, whispering and watching her.

"Don't even pay attention to Lindsay," Caitlin said. "She just knows she's got competition now."

Anna shrugged. "If you say so," she said.

"Trust me, you'll be playing before the end of the game," Caitlin said.

Once the game had started, Anna started to feel better. She loved watching football almost as much as she loved playing it.

Caitlin and Bethany each scored one goal. After Anna had watched Lindsay make some very nice saves, she had to admit that Lindsay was pretty great in goal.

With only a couple of minutes left, Coach Suzy put her hand on Anna's shoulder. "Okay, Anna," the coach said. "Let's see what you've got."

Anna looked up. "You want me in? Now?" Anna asked.

Coach Suzy nodded. "Yes," she said. Then she called, "Lindsay, take a seat."

Lindsay looked over at the sidelines and shot the coach a confused look. Coach Suzy waved her over, and she shrugged and jogged towards the bench.

Anna got to her feet. Smiling, she took over at goal. She passed Lindsay on the way. "Good luck, Second String," Lindsay said with a sneer.

Anna ignored her and took her place in front of the goal.

"Okay," she thought. "Here we go. Time to show these East Moor girls what you're made of." She didn't have to wait long.

The other team's central midfielder was driving with both wings, and a shot would be coming soon.

The midfielder sold Alicia a dummy. Then she passed around Jasmine to the right wing.

"Here she comes," Anna said to herself. She was ready to spring at the shot.

Then it came. Anna watched the girl's feet closely. She pulled back, looking left and low, but Anna saw her foot turning. The girl was definitely shooting to the right. There was no doubt about it.

Anna dived to her right just as the shot took off. The ball hit her in the stomach, and she hugged it against herself.

Blocked!

"Woo!" Bethany called from midpitch. "Nice save, Reed!"

Anna didn't take the time to celebrate. She immediately got to her feet, held the ball in both hands, and drew back to kick.

Anna's kick was long and high. By the time it hit the ground, the game was over.

"Great save, Anna," Coach Suzy said when the players returned to the bench after the final whistle.

"Thanks, Coach Suzy," Anna replied, smiling.

She grabbed a towel from the bench and wiped her face. When she pulled the towel away, Coach Suzy had walked off.

Lindsay and Alicia were standing there. They glared at Anna.

"It didn't even matter," Alicia told Anna. "We would have won even if they scored."

"Yeah," added Lindsay. "Besides, it was just a lucky leap . . . Second String."

CHAPTER 9

IMPOSSIBLE

The next game was a few days later. Before the game, Coach Suzy walked back and forth with her clipboard. All the East Moor players sat on the bench.

"You girls have been looking great in practice," Coach Suzy said. "Today we're going to try a few new things."

The coach listed a few new positions and switched some players around. Caitlin was getting a shot in midfield.

"Nice job, Caitlin," Bethany said. "You'll do great."

"Thanks," Caitlin replied.

"And starting in goal," Coach Suzy went on, "let's see Anna today."

Lindsay jumped up. "What?" she yelled. "After my perfect game the other day?"

"Take a seat, please, Lindsay," Coach Suzy said without looking up. "Let's not compete with our teammates, okay?"

Lindsay sat back on the bench. "This is completely unfair," she muttered to herself. Alicia sat down next to her and glared at Anna.

"Don't let them get to you," Caitlin said. "Just play your best."

Coach Suzy blew her whistle. "All right," she said. "Let's do this!"

The game was very close. After thirty minutes, the score was still 0–0. Anna had blocked a few shots, and Bethany and Caitlin had each been stopped by the other team's goalie a couple of times. Something big would have to happen soon.

Caitlin tried a side pass to Bethany, but the other team got it. Soon the other team was driving down the pitch. Jasmine tried to cut them off, but the other team's wing made a great pass clear across the pitch.

"Keep it away!" Anna called up to her defence. Alicia looked back at Anna and smirked.

"What's she smiling about?" Anna wondered.

Then, just as the other team's offence was about to corner themselves out of shot range, Alicia tumbled.

"Whoa!" Alicia cried as she hit the ground.

The other team's offence suddenly had nothing between them and Anna's goal. All three players charged her. Jasmine couldn't get over to cover Alicia's position in time. It would all be up to Anna.

The midfielder pulled back to shoot, but as Anna watched her feet, she knew she would pass instead. Now the wing had the ball, and she was moving in fast on the right. Anna turned to face her, expecting a shot, but the wing passed across the crease.

Anna jumped to her left, but they were too fast for her. The other wing pulled back and shot behind Anna. She tried to change directions, but in midair, it was impossible.

"Goal!" the referee called out.

★ CHAPTER 10 ★

JUST SLIPPED?

Anna got to her feet and brushed off her jersey and shorts. Alicia was standing at the top of the crease, smiling at her.

"Well done, Second String," Alicia said. "Thanks for losing the game for us."

"Her?" Bethany yelled as she stormed downpitch. "You're blaming her for losing the game for us? What did you do, Alicia? Slip on a banana peel or something?"

Alicia smiled nervously and looked around. "What . . . what are you talking about?" she asked.

"We all saw you take a dive," Jasmine said. "Was it just to make Anna look stupid?"

"I did not take a dive," Alicia said. "I just slipped."

Anna looked over at the bench. Lindsay was hanging her head and Coach Suzy was heading towards Alicia, Bethany, and Jasmine on the pitch.

A moment later, Sophie was taking Alicia's place on defence.

"Anna, don't worry about that goal," Sophie said. "Coach Suzy is angry at Alicia. Even Lindsay seems angry at her."

"Really?" Anna asked. "Even Lindsay?"

Sophie nodded as play started at midpitch. "Yep," she said, jogging away to join the game in action. "Lindsay said something about not wanting to lose a game just so she could start again."

Anna was shocked. Could it be that Lindsay cared enough about her team to give Anna a fair chance?

Bethany was fired up after Alicia's fall. She immediately drove for the other goal and made a great shot around one defender, fooling their goalie completely. The score was 1–1. A few minutes later, Jasmine got a pass and kicked the ball up to Caitlin. Caitlin scored, making the score 2–1 to East Moor.

There were only a few seconds left. "We can win this!" Anna shouted, clapping.

But the other team wasn't ready to lose yet. Their offence started driving up the pitch. Their central midfielder sold Jasmine a dummy and passed it off to their right wing. Sophie tried to steal the ball, but the other team's right wing passed it right between her legs!

"Uh-oh," Anna thought. "They want to tie this game really badly."

Anna crouched and watched the offence approach. "Here we go again," she mumbled. She was facing their offence alone, for the second time in one game.

The midfielder passed it off to the wing, just like last time. Anna stayed ready. The wing passed it fast and hard across the crease to the other wing, just like last time.

This time, Anna didn't jump too soon. She watched the wing's feet.

At the exact right moment, as the ball went high and to the right, Anna bounced. She knocked the ball with the tip of her fingers and made the save.

"Yes!" she cried, as she hit the ground.

"Nice save, Anna!" Bethany called.

"We won!" Jasmine added, pumping her fist.

Anna got to her feet and dusted herself off. The students and parents in the stands went crazy cheering for her great save.

"Nice save, Second String," Lindsay said as the whole team gathered in the crease to celebrate. "I mean, Anna. Nice save."

Anna smiled at her. "Thanks, Lindsay," she said. "Hope you won't mind sharing this goal with me for the rest of the season."

"I'll be happy to," Lindsay said. "And I'm sorry." She raised her hand for Anna to slap.

"Don't worry about it," Anna said, slapping Lindsay's hand and smiling. "After all, we're on the same team now, right?"

ABOUT THE AUTHOR

Eric Stevens is studying to become an English teacher. Some of his favourite things include pizza, playing computer games, watching cookery programmes on TV, cycling, and trying new restaurants. Olives are one of his least favourite things.

ABOUT THE ILLUSTRATOR

When Tuesday Mourning was a little girl, she knew she wanted to be an artist when she grew up. Now, she is an illustrator who is especially keen on working on books for children and teenagers. When she isn't illustrating, Tuesday loves spending time with her husband, who is an actor, and their son, Atticus.

GLOSSARY

competition   when someone or something is your competition, you are competing with them, or you are both trying to get the same thing

enemies   those you are fighting against

funding   money for something

immediately   right away

psychic   someone who can tell what will happen in the future

rival   someone whom you are competing against

second string   member of a group that is not chosen first

FOOTBALL WORDS YOU SHOULD KNOW

boundaries   lines on the edge of the football pitch

crease   area near the goal

defender   person playing defence, trying to keep the other team from scoring

drill   practice something by doing it over and over

goalie   person whose role is to stop the other team from scoring by blocking their shots

kick-off   at the beginning of the game, the kick-off decides which team has control of the ball

line-up   list of which person will be playing which position

midfield   middle part of the pitch

midfielder   one of the players whose job is to score points

offence   team that is attacking or trying to score, or the players whose job it is to score

referee   someone who supervises a sports match and makes sure that all the players follow the rules

sell a dummy   pretend to go one way but intending to go another

starting player   one of the players who are first on the pitch

wing   an attacking player

DISCUSSION QUESTIONS

1. At Gladstone School, the only option for girls' football was to join the East Moor team. Can you think of other ways that the girls in this book could have played football, without having to join another school's team?

2. If you had to choose between joining another school's team or quitting your favourite sport, which would you pick? Explain your answer.

3. How do you think the girls at East Moor Secondary School felt to have new girls joining their team?

WRITING PROMPTS

1. Have you ever had to co-operate with someone from a rival team or group? How did you make it work? What happened? Write about it.

2. Has anyone ever been mean to you on a sports team or in another group? Write about what happened.

3. At the end of this book, Anna and Lindsay are nice to each other. What do you think happens after that? Write a page about what happens the next time that Anna and Lindsay see each other.

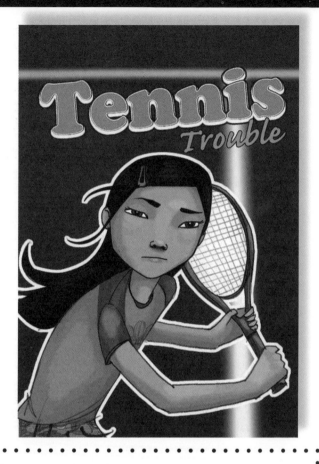

Alexis is on the school tennis team. She's thrilled, but some older girls are out to make it a terrible year for her. Can she keep up her self-confidence and step up to the net, or will she let the girls get to her and lose everything?

Jenny knows she should stay away from the water when a storm heads for the coast of Cornwall, but Abby and Sarah think surfing in the storm will be amazing. Who will save them when the waves get out of control?

FIND OUT MORE

Books

Fantastic Football, Clive Gifford (Oxford University Press, 2010)

Football Mad, John Goodwin, Alan Macdonald, and Helen Pielechaty (Oxford University Press, 2008)

Football Skills, Clive Gifford (Kingfisher Books, 2005)

Websites

www.thefa.com/Womens
Find out everything you need to know about the Football Association and women's football.

www.girlsinfootball.co.uk
This useful website has lots of information and advice on skills for keen football players.